Wishing
I Was
Fishing

by Eva Wells

Illustrated by Chandra Dale

Beaver's Pond Press, Inc.

Edina, Minnesota

To Ryan-
Eva Wells
May 2008

Illustrated by Chandra Dale

ISBN 13: 978-1-59298-168-7
ISBN 10: 1-59298-168-2

Library of Congress Catalog Number: 2006935998

Printed in the United States of America

First Printing: January 2007
10 09 08 07 06   5 4 3 2 1

Beaver's Pond Press, Inc.

7104 Ohms Lane, Suite 216
Edina, MN 55439
(952) 829-8818
www.BeaversPondPress.com

To order, visit www.BookHouseFulfillment.com
or call 1-800-901-3480. Quantity discounts available.

To my parents, who always supported my dreams,
and to Peter, Alex, and Jack, my three fishermen
ERW

To the Wells family for all of their help,
and to my family, Michael, Noah and Audra,
for their love, patience and support
CD

The snow is melting in our yard.

Soon my dad will be working hard…

outside with me on our big boat. We'll fix it up so it can float.

I'll help him make the motor run and shine it up under the sun.

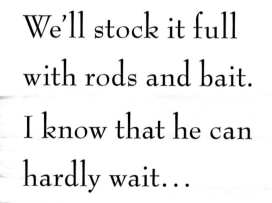

We'll stock it full
with rods and bait.
I know that he can
hardly wait…

to join the truck and boat parade

down at the boat launch in the shade.

He'll gently back the trailer in and watch the boat glide with a grin.

I'll hold the rope and watch him park, and Sam, our dog, will start to bark.

She'll know it's time to jump inside the boat to go for our first ride.

Then Dad will march down on the dock
and he will see me skip a rock.

I'll close my life vest with a snap,
and Dad will turn his baseball cap...

as we prepare to cross the lake

full throttle with a great big wake.

We'll cut the waves and I will jump

when Dad's boat skips them with a bump.

The wind will blow across my face until we find the perfect place...

with lily pads and weeds
so green, the calmest place
you've ever seen!

I'll put a minnow on my
hook and throw it toward
the little brook…

back in the corner of the bay where all the big fish swim and play.

Then Dad will cast his fishing line
under the tree right next to mine,

and we will sit so still and wait
for hungry fish to bite our bait.

My bobber will bounce by the shore.

Soon I won't see it anymore.

I'll jerk my line and reel it fast. The greatest part has come at last!

My dad will smile and so will I as my fish flies into the sky.

Inside the boat he'll flip and
flop. We'll throw him back
with a KERPLOP!

Then once again I'll grab my bait
and sit back down and start to wait.

We'll catch one hundred fish that day—at least that's what my dad will say.

But now I guess
it's time for bed,
so as the pillow
hits my head…

I'll close my eyes and make a wish that I will catch...

the BIGGEST fish!

About the Author
Eva Wells lives in Woodbury, Minnesota with her husband and two sons. She was raised in Saint Paul, Minnesota, and received a Bachelor of Arts in Accounting and Spanish from Concordia College in Moorhead, Minnesota. She is a CPA with an MBA from Metropolitan State University.

About the Illustrator
Chandra Dale grew up in Saint Paul, Minnesota. She holds a Bachelor of Fine Arts in Graphic Design from Mankato State University (now Minnesota State), as well as an Associate of Arts from Bethany Lutheran College, Mankato, Minnesota. She lives in Port St. Lucie, Florida with her husband and two children.